Chicklet's Dream

LINDA CROW CADEN

Archway Publishing books may be ordered through booksellers or by contacting:

Archway Publishing
1663 Liberty Drive
Bloomington, IN 47403
www.archwaypublishing.com
1 (888) 242-5904

Because of the dynamic nature of the Internet, any web addresses or links contained in this book may have changed since publication and may no longer be valid. The views expressed in this work are solely those of the author and do not necessarily reflect the views of the publisher, and the publisher hereby disclaims any responsibility for them.

Any people depicted in stock imagery provided by Thinkstock are models, and such images are being used for illustrative purposes only.
Certain stock imagery © Thinkstock.

ISBN: 978-1-4808-1862-0 (sc)
ISBN: 978-1-4808-1863-7 (hc)
ISBN: 978-1-4808-1864-4 (e)

Library of Congress Control Number: 2015909980

Print information available on the last page.

Archway Publishing rev. date: 07/30/2015

Preface

Within every photo I take, there seems to be a story, just waiting to be told. The tale that emerged from the pictures in this book sounded perfect for children. Little Chicklet is discovering his world, just as readers are discovering theirs.

My hope is that this adventure will not only entertain, but also introduce children to the wonderful world of birds. Ideally, it will encourage an appreciation for some of the fascinating creatures with whom we share this planet.

Linda Crow Caden
Ponte Vedra Beach, Florida
June 2015

Now, let's meet Little Chicklet...

To John. Without you, this story would still be trapped in the photographs.

Chicklet was dreaming.
Again.
His eyes were closed but he
was making little peeping
sounds, and fluttering his
little wings. His tummy was
grumbling too.

He was dreaming of
flying.
Flying with a fish in his
little beak.
Because most of all,
Chicklet was hungry.
Again.

Chicklet was a little shorebird called a tern.

A Royal Tern.

He lived in the tall grasses in the dunes on the beach. There were many other little Royal Tern chicks and their families too. It was safe. It was comfy. It was home.

So Chicklet was dreaming his flying dream when suddenly his eyes popped open and his mouth popped open and he peeped, "I'm huuuuuun-gry."

Usually when he did this his mom would give him some food.

Yum.

Hmmmmm.

No mom. No food.

Lots of other birds were around, but not HIS mom or HIS dad.

So he peeped again, but this time a very very very loud peep.

"I'm huuuuuun-gry, please!"

This time he added *please*. *Always a good idea,* he thought to himself.

No luck.

So he got up and started looking around. He discovered that his mom had left him a note that said:

Chicklet thought, *Oh, goody! Fish for breakfast!*

So he and his friends hopped down the dune.

They headed for the water, where his mom would catch wonderful, tasty fish.

Gone fishin.
B back soon.
XOX,
Mom

Chicklet hopped on toward the water's edge and he waited...

And waited...

And waited.

Finally he thought, *Fishing can't be that hard. I can do it too!* So he hopped a little farther out and looked for a fish to catch.

He saw a small Sandpiper in the shallow, bubbly water who looked like he might have food.

"Do you have a fish??" asked Chicklet hopefully.

"No fishy. Just itchy," said the Sandpiper.

Hmmm, this wasn't going to be so easy.

He did see little fish in the water, but they swam away very fast.

How was he ever going to catch one?

Who should he ask?

Chicklet saw Bob in the crowd, and hopped over to him.
Bob was his best best friend.
He was a little older and
wiser, and a lot taller.
When Chicklet looked at Bob,
he could really see why they
were called Royal Terns.
Bob already was growing a
black crown on his head.
Very royal. Kind of spikey.
Chicklet loved it.

"Hey Bob, just exactly how do you fish?" asked Chicklet.
"I'm not sure. I'm not that much older than you are. Let's watch
that bird over there," said Bob.

It was a Willet in the water.

The Willet walked very carefully, very stealthily, in the surf. Suddenly, the Willet poked his bill down in the sand and up he came with a snail!

"Uh, like that," said Bob.
"You have to be really fast, little Chicklet," said the Willet.
That could be a problem. He wasn't fast at anything. Not yet anyway.

Suddenly there was a big splashing commotion in the deep water.
Splashing and diving and flapping of wings!
It was a flock of pelicans, and they were doing some serious fishing!

Before Chicklet could catch their attention, the pelicans scooped up their fish in their pouches, and flew away.
They soared high in the sky like airplanes.

Chicklet thought, Oh, boy. Not only do I have to be really fast, I also need to be a really good swimmer. This could be a big problem.
He was talking to Bob about it when somebody shouted,
"Look up! Look up!"
"Watch out! Watch out!"
"Eeeeeeeeeeeek!"

What is that!?
thought Chicklet.

It was an Osprey, flying high
and diving low to catch a
fish with his looonnng, pointy
talons. He grabbed a fish and
flew away.

FAST.

Little Chicklet thought, *Whew! At first I thought that guy was coming my way! Lucky for me he was hungry for fish, not little Chicklets.*
I wish I were fast. I wish I could swim. I wish I could dive like that Osprey.
I'd fly up up up and then down down down!
I could definitely find food that way.
And Little Chicklet began to day-dream... Up up up and down down down...
As he flapped his little wings, he dreamed he was bigger and stronger.

I can do this,
thought Chicklet,
fluttering his
wings with great
determination.

And pretty soon...

...he was flying!

He was soaring!

His imagination was so powerful that Chicklet actually thought
he was flying. This was an amazing thing, because little chicks
aren't strong enough to fly. Not until they get bigger.

"Hey, Bobby. I just thought I saw Chicklet flying up there."

"No way......."

"Uh-yep. There he goes."

So, Chicklet was imagining he was flying! As he was moving away
from the ocean's edge he looked and looked for water where
fish might be swimming.

Soon he came to a beautiful area of ponds and canals and islands of trees.

As he got closer, he could see a mama bird and three chicks.

Boy, were they noisy.

"Hi! I'm Chicklet! What kinds of birds are you?"

"We are Great White Herons."

The mama had a long yellow beak, and looked like she would be a very
good fisherman, so Chicklet asked her if she was going to go fishing.

Her chicks sounded very hungry too.

"No, not now. Trying to get these little ones to settle down," she said.

Hmmm. No fish here. Guess I'll move on.

Next he passed a nest of blue and brown birds. "Hi! I'm Chicklet! Who are you?"

"We are Tri-Colored Herons," said the mama, "and my chicks are very hungry."

"And that's a little Snowy Egret chick down there. She's so hungry her tongue is hanging out!"

Tell me about it, whispered Chicklet to himself.

Then he saw a beautiful pink bird flying above him. And two more in the trees nearby.

"Hi. I'm Chicklet!
I love your pretty pink feathers!
And that's a very unusual shaped bill you have there.
Uh, by the way, are you going fishing soon?" he said hopefully. Maybe he could tag along.
"No. We're TRYING to build a nest," they said.
"Looks hard," said Chicklet, secretly hoping they would change their minds and go fishing instead. They were really struggling with that stick.
"Well, it IS hard! Especially when you have this odd shaped bill like we do.

We're Roseate Spoonbills, OK?
The pink is nice, but these bills have got to go. And it's even harder to talk AND hold sticks, if you know what I mean," mumbled the Spoonbill.
"Well, good luck," said little Chicklet, thinking that SOMEBODY was a grumpity grump, and he hopped on.

Chicklet was seeing many white birds, and this male Great Egret might be the best of all. He was spreading his tail and curving his neck in some kind of dance. He was beautiful!

"You are so attractive, Mr. Great Egret! Shake your tail feathers!" sang Chicklet.

"Thanks. I've been doing this all day, hoping my girlfriend would see me," said the Great Egret.

I'm sure she will, thought Chicklet. *He's pretty hard to miss.*

"HEY. HEY. HEY. Who are you???" said two white birds on a branch. "We haven't seen you before."
"I'm Chicklet! Who are you?"
"We are Cattle Egrets," they said in unison.
"Hmmm. Are you related to cows?" asked Chicklet cautiously.
"What!? Cows?? That's not funny.
No! We're BIRDS, not COWS. ...Related to cows...."
Oh, boy, oh, boy, oh, boy, oh, boy. Time to get out of here, thought Chicklet.

He was a little distracted, thinking about that odd couple of Cattle Egret BIRDS, when he heard a great flapping of wings and looked up to see...

Eeeeeek! A ginormous black and white bird zooming directly toward him!

"No!
Please!
I'm not edible!
Just feathers!
Nothing tasty here!"
squeaked Chicklet.
Luckily, the big bird
swooped away.

Whew. That was close. But there were more birds like that in the next tree! They were HUGE!

Actually, they looked much less scary than that dinosaurus birdarus that almost attacked him. But they were big and bald, and had really long beaks.

"Excuse me," Chicklet said, very politely, just in case they were grumpity grumps too.

"You wouldn't by any small slight possible chance be going fishing, would you?"

"Fishing? No.

"We--are--Wood Storks!
Big and Bald and Pret-ty!
We--are--Wood Storks!
Big and Bald and Pret-ty!"
At the end of the song they'd clack their beaks together and start all over again.

Chicklet moved on, and they didn't even seem to notice, so engrossed were they in their song. It WAS kind of catchy.

Wow! Look in that pond over there. I know who that is. It's another Great Egret! Why is he standing so still and so silent as he peers into the water? Chicklet was about to shout out a big Helllllooooo when the Egret said,

"Shhhhh! I've been trying to catch a fish all morning. I must have quiet and complete stillness!"
So Chicklet tip-toed by, as quietly as he could, thinking what a nice lunch that might have been.

Just then a Great Blue Heron called to him,
"Hey, little Chicklet. See that log floating in the water back behind me?"

"Yes," chirped Chicklet. He did see the log. It was not exactly like other logs he knew, but, OK. "Yes. A log."

"Well, I've got a riddle for you. When is a log not a log?" said the Great Blue, mischievously.

"Uh...When?" said Chicklet. He had no idea where this was going.

"When it's an alligator!" shrieked the Heron, throwing up his head in laughter.

"That doesn't make sense," said Chicklet.

"Well, sonny, make sense of this. That LOG, yes, that very one right there, is an alligator. And his beady little eye is focused on chicklet drumettes. He'll tackle you in a flash, and you'll be lunch for HIM."

"Well. Gotta scoot! Nice chatting with you. Keep up those riddles," said Chicklet as he got out of there as fast as his little legs would take him.

"Little Chicklet, come over here," said a black bird with silver wings, spread out like he was about to take off.

"Oh, no. There might be alligators there!" said Chicklet.

"Well, you are right to be cautious. But there are no gators here. Just a Snake Bird!"

"Snake Bird! Where??" said Chicklet. *What a dangerous place.*

"Me! Snake Bird. Anhinga. Whatever. I look like a snake to some people with my long neck coming out of the water. But as for gators, I checked the area. All clear. Drying my wings now. I get so wet when I dive for a tasty fish. Just had a big one."

"Fish? Oh, my. Is there any left?" asked Chicklet meekly.

"Nope. Not a bite. Speared it. Tossed it up in the air. Caught it quick. Sucked it down in... let's see...about 3 gulps. Down the hatch. Gone. Done. Finished. Why?"

"Oh, no reason," said Little Chicklet, and he trudged on, a little slower than before, with his head hanging low. It was a most dejected hop.

"Boo!"

Chicklet jumped about 3 inches off the ground, he was so surprised.
"Boo Hoo!" said a skinny necked chick, as he popped his head out of
the leaves.
It was one of those Tri-Colored Heron chicks, out of his nest.
Very scary. Very scary. I am soooo scared, thought Chicklet.
This place is getting kind of weird. Maybe I should just hop on.
And so he did.

How about this wetland place? Yes! There's someone!
It's a wading bird with the perfect curved pink bill for finding
little nibbles of things, thought Chicklet.

"What beautiful blue eyes you
have!" he peeped to the bird.
"What? Why thank you, little
guy. I must agree, if I do say
so myself.
I'm an Ibis.
That's EYE-bis.
Yes, I am," he said pompously,
as he preened at his reflection
in the water.
"I see," said Chicklet, nodding

agreeably. "Any luck probing in there?"
But the Ibis already had his bill back in the mud, digging busily,
and couldn't hear Chicklet's little voice.
So Chicklet sauntered on, mumbling in his deepest Chicklet voice,
"I'm an I-bis. That's EYE-bis. EYE-EYE-EYE-bis."

What was that sound?

Chicklet heard a high, piercing, whistling call, far above him.

He looked up and spotted an Osprey in a pine tree, with a fish of course. It reminded him of the first Osprey he had ever seen. The one back home, diving and fishing where he lived. He thought about his

buddies on the beach, and his family. He was getting homesick, and maybe a little tired, not to mention the "h" word.

The Osprey gave him the evil eye, and Chicklet peeped a little "Eeeeek."

"Hmmmm," Chicklet sighed.

He didn't have talons to grab a fish like the Osprey.

Didn't have a curved beak like the Ibis to dig for yummy things in the sand.

He wasn't fast like the Willet.

He didn't have a pointy beak to spear a fish like the Anhinga.

And he couldn't fly.

"Oh, what a wonderful thing it would be if I really could fly," he said dreamily.

He squinted up his little eyes, and flapped his little wings, and whispered, "up and down, up and down," and pretty soon...he was flying again!

The dream was so vivid.

He was really into it, swooping and diving, soaring and gliding!

But there was some annoying laughter in the background that kept getting louder and louder.

It was a flock of Laughing Gulls, and they were laughing at HIM.

"HA HA HA.

A chicklet can't fly.

A chicklet can't fly.

My oh my. A chicklet can't fly!"

And with that, Chicklet woke up on the sand, amid thousands of birds on the beach. *Plop.*

He was dazed and confused. The gulls had flown away, but was somebody else calling his name?
"Chicklet! Chicklet!"

Chicklet looked here and there. He looked up and down. "Chicklet! Chicklet!" Who's calling me??

"Mom! You're back! And you caught lunch!"

"Yes I did, sweetie. Here you go."

"I think I got it," he said in a tiny voice.

This was a huge fish. Almost as big as he was. How was he going to swallow it?

"Hold your head up and stretch your neck like this," said his friend, Bob.

"Arrrghhh. I think I got it," he said again, secretly hoping it wouldn't get stuck.

Suddenly, he swallowed it right down.

Gulp.

Wow. That's better.

Yum!

"Thanks, Mom."

"Chicklet. I've been looking and looking for you.
Where have you been this morning?" asked his mom. His friends
wanted to know too.
Chicklet peeped with delight, and said,
"Come on, everybody. Have I got a story for you!"

THE END

CPSIA information can be obtained
at www.ICGtesting.com
Printed in the USA
BVOW10*0907130416

443566BV00014B/19/P

9 781480 818637